The Girl On The Moon

Written by: Denean Powell
Illustrated by: Justin Green

Paperback edition: January 2021

ISBN 978-1-09836-196-9

Printed in the United States of America."

This book is dedicated to the two people that gave me the title "Mommy" - Soleil and Saigan. You two provide my beating heart with everything that it needs to exist on this earth. My heart is filled with love and I'm thankful that you two make it full!

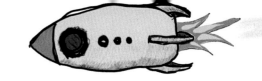

I HAVE TO COME OFF THE MOON
AND JOIN MY FAMILY AGAIN.

WHEN I AM ON THE MOON,
I MISS OUT ON SO MUCH.

4

Due
Tomorrow

WHEN WORKING ON HOMEWORK....

I VISIT THE MOON
AND MY HOMEWORK IS NEVER
FINISHED.

WHILE STUDYING SPELLING WORDS...

I VISIT THE MOON
AND MY GRADES ARE NOT THE BEST.

CLASSROOM

WHEN LISTENING TO A LESSON IN CLASS...

I VISIT THE MOON
AND I SIMPLY MISS OUT ON
IMPORTANT DETAILS.

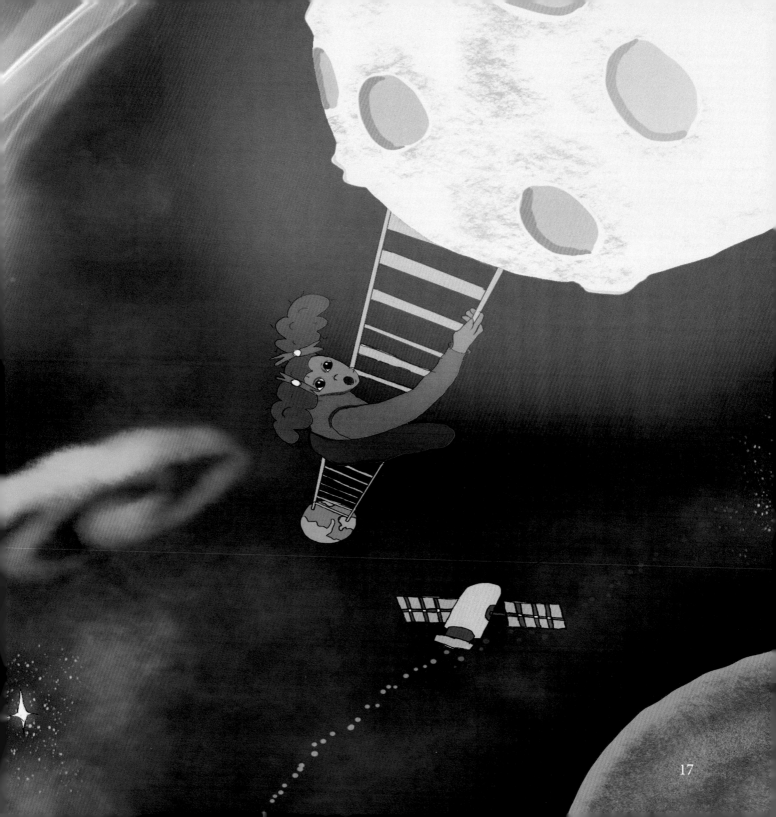

WHILE WALKING THE DOG...

I VISIT THE MOON
AND MY DOG ENDS UP WALKING ME.

WHILE TAKING A BATH...

23

I VISIT THE MOON
AND TEN MINUTES TURNS INTO TWO HOURS,
LEAVING MY SKIN LOOKING LIKE A PRUNE.

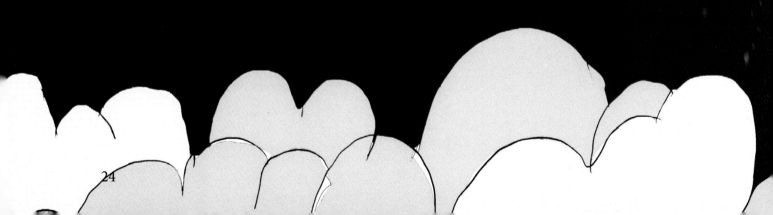

WHILE TYING MY SHOES...

I VISIT THE MOON
AND MY SHOES END UP
GETTING TIED TOGETHER.

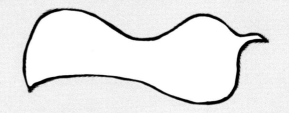

WHILE WAITING FOR THE SCHOOL BUS...

I VISIT THE MOON
AND I END UP MISSING MY BUS.

DURING LUNCH TIME...

I VISIT THE MOON
AND I MISS OUT ON EATING MY LUNCH.

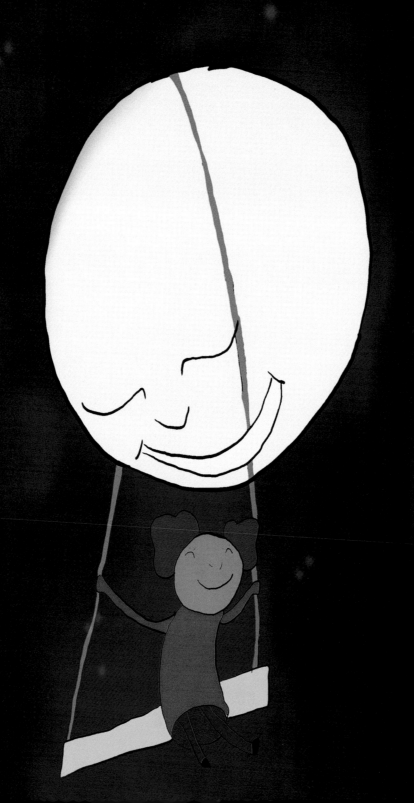

WHILE GROCERY SHOPPING

FOR MY

GRANDMOTHER....

I VISIT THE MOON
AND I END UP WANDERING AROUND THE
SUPERMARKET WITH AN EMPTY SHOPPING CART.

lessons with deedee!!!

1. CAN YOU RECALL A TIME YOU FELT LIKE YOU WERE ON THE MOON?

2. WHAT CAN HAPPEN IF YOU VISIT THE MOON WHILE STUDYING?

3. WHAT CAN HAPPEN IF YOU VISIT THE MOON WHILE TYING YOUR SHOES?

4. DOES THE GIRL ON THE MOON GET THINGS DONE WHEN VISITING THE MOON?

5. WHY IS IT IMPORTANT TO COME OFF THE MOON?

FACTS ABOUT SICKLE CELL

SICKLE CELL ANEMIA IS A RED BLOOD CELL DISORDER. THE DISEASE IS INHERITED WHEN TWO PARENTS HAVE SICKLE CELL TRAIT.

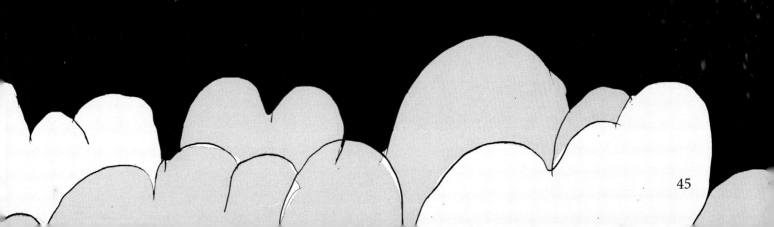

The Girl on The Moon is Denean's first published children's book. Denean's love for writing began during her childhood. As a child, Denean loved writing songs, poems, and plays. Denean's favorite book was A Light in the Attic, by Shel Silverstein. While working in the behavioral/mental health field, Denean was inspired by the children she met along the way. Denean resides in Pennsylvania with her two loving daughters. When Denean is not writing, she enjoys spending time with her two daughters, eating spicy food, listening to music, and working with children.

THE END